P9-BZH-403
3 9048 07643468 1

SSF

W
S.S.F. Public Library
West Orange
840 West Orange Ave.
South San Francisco, CA 94080

MAR 2010

GAYLORD

OUNCE DICE TRICE

THE NEW YORK REVIEW CHILDREN'S COLLECTION
NEW YORK

OUNCE DICE TRICE

BY ALASTAIR REID

DRAWINGS BY BEN SHAHN

THIS IS A NEW YORK REVIEW BOOK
PUBLISHED BY THE NEW YORK REVIEW OF BOOKS

Text copyright © 1958 by Alastair Reid
Illustrations © 1958 by the Estate of Ben Shahn
All rights reserved.

Ben Shahn's illustrations are reproduced under license from VAGA, New York, NY

Published in the United States of America by
New York Review Books, 435 Hudson Street, New York, NY 10014
www.nyrb.com

Library of Congress Cataloging-in-Publication Data

Reid, Alastair, 1926–
Ounce, dice, trice / by Alastair Reid ; illustrated by Ben Shahn.
p. cm. — (New York Review Books children's collection)
ISBN 978-1-59017-320-6 (alk. paper)
1. Vocabulary—Humor. 2. Wit and humor, Juvenile. I. Shahn, Ben, 1898–1969. II. Title.
PR6035.E4O8 2009
428.102'07—dc22
2008050325

ISBN 978-1-59017-320-6

Cover design by Louise Fili Ltd.

Printed in the United States on acid-free paper.
3 5 7 9 10 8 6 4

Introduction

This book is an odd collection of words and names, to amuse and amaze you.

Words have a sound and shape, in addition to their meanings. Sometimes the sound is *the meaning. If you take a word like BALLOON and say it aloud seven or eight times, you will grow quite dizzy with it. All the words here are meant to be said aloud, over and over, for your own delight. If you want to know more about their meanings, ask a dictionary.*

In the book, too, you will find some curiosities, old words no longer in use, new words which ought to exist if they do not, private family words which deserve to be better known. And if you grow to love words for their own sake, you will begin to collect words for yourself, and you will be grateful, as I am, to all the people who collect odd words and edit odd dictionaries, out of sheer astonishment and affection.

For Michael's Sake

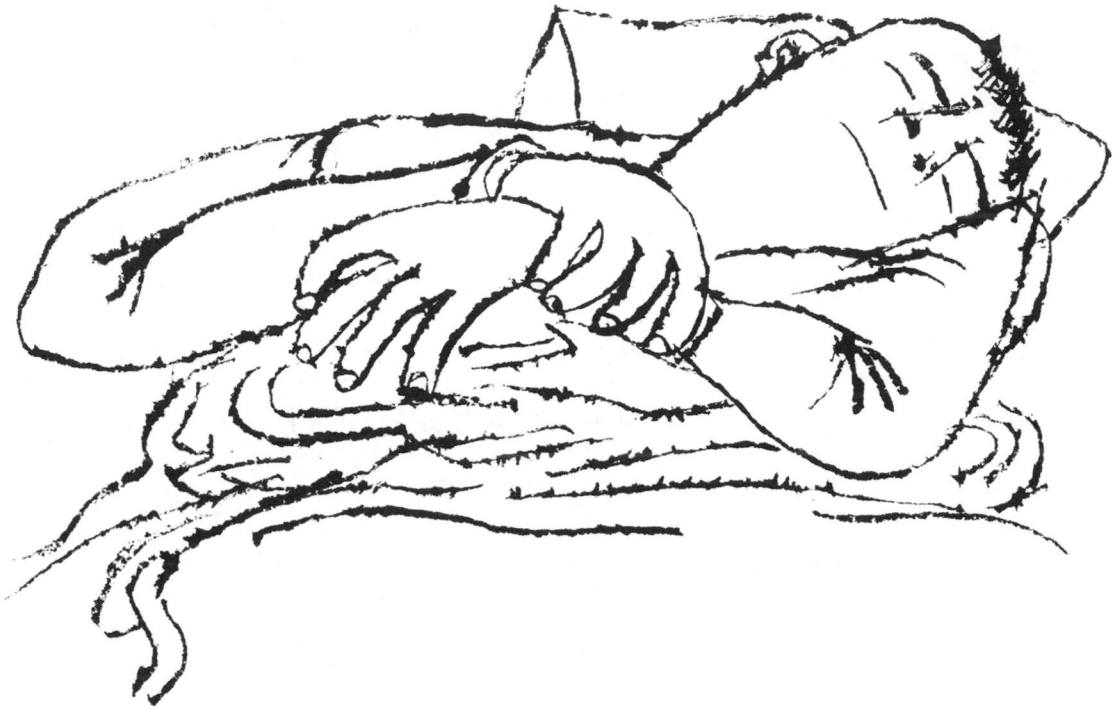

The way to get the feel of words is to begin with a sound and let it grow. ZZZZ is the sound of someone sleeping. From it, you easily move to BUZZ and DIZZY, and soon you have a list.

ZZZZ

BUZZ

DIZZY

FIZZLE

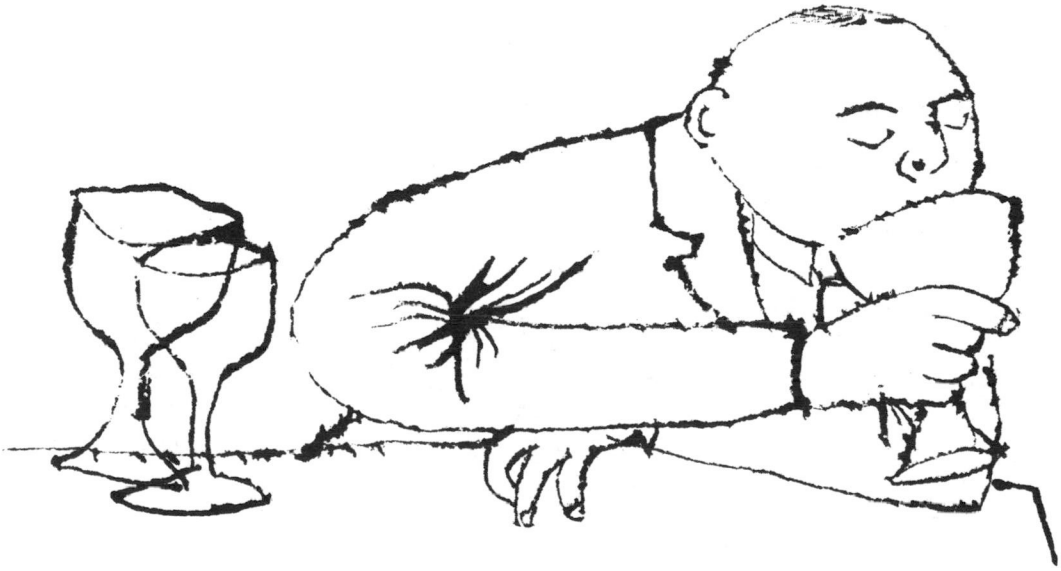

GUZZLE

BUZZARD

BAMBOOZLE

Or begin with OG
and see what happens.

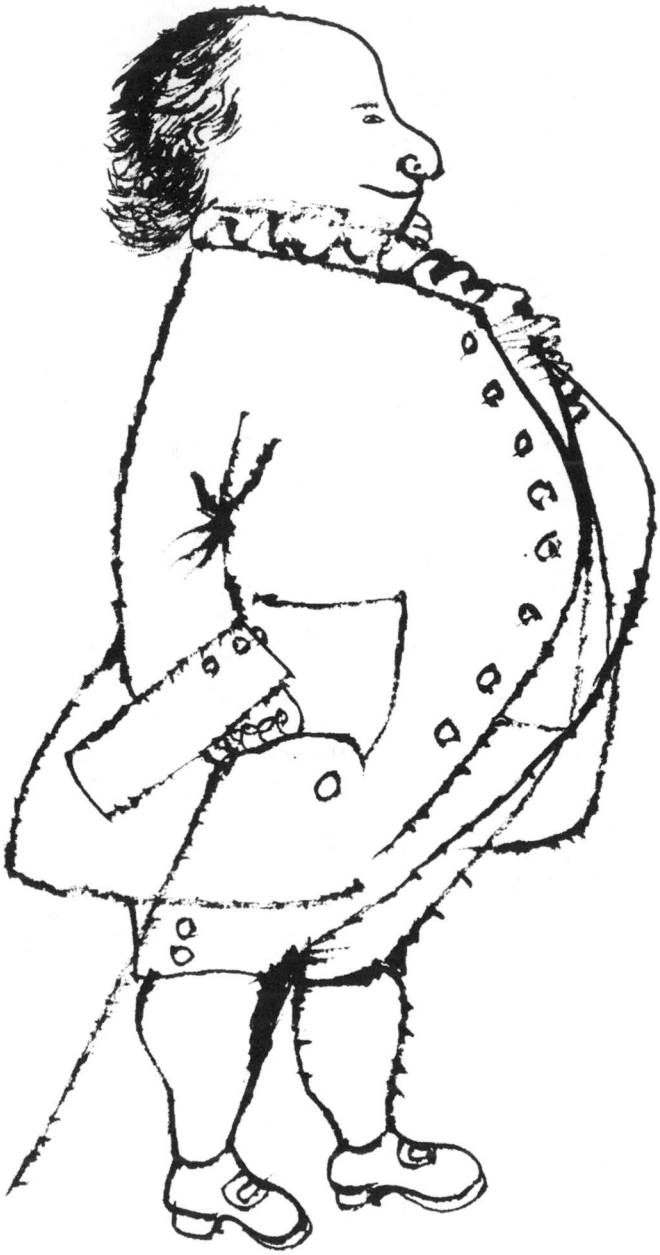

OG

FROG

OGLED

GOGGLE

GROGGY

TOBOGGAN

HEDGEHOG

And then you can make other lists, by gathering together words for noises or nightmares or things beginning with Q. Here are some lists to guide you.

LIGHT WORDS

(to be said in windy or singing moods)

ARIEL

WILLOW

SPINNAKER

WHIRR

LISSOM

SIBILANT

PETTICOAT

NIMBLE

NIB

HEAVY WORDS

(to be used in gloom or bad weather)

DUFFLE

BLUNDERBUSS

GALOSHES

BOWL

BEFUDDLED

MUGWUMP

PUMPKIN

CRUMB

BLOB

WORDS TO BE SAID ON THE MOVE

FLIT

FLUCTUATE

WOBBLE

WIGGLE

SHIVER

TIPTOE

PIROUETTE

TWIRL

TEETER

ODD WORDS

(to be spoken out loud, for fun)

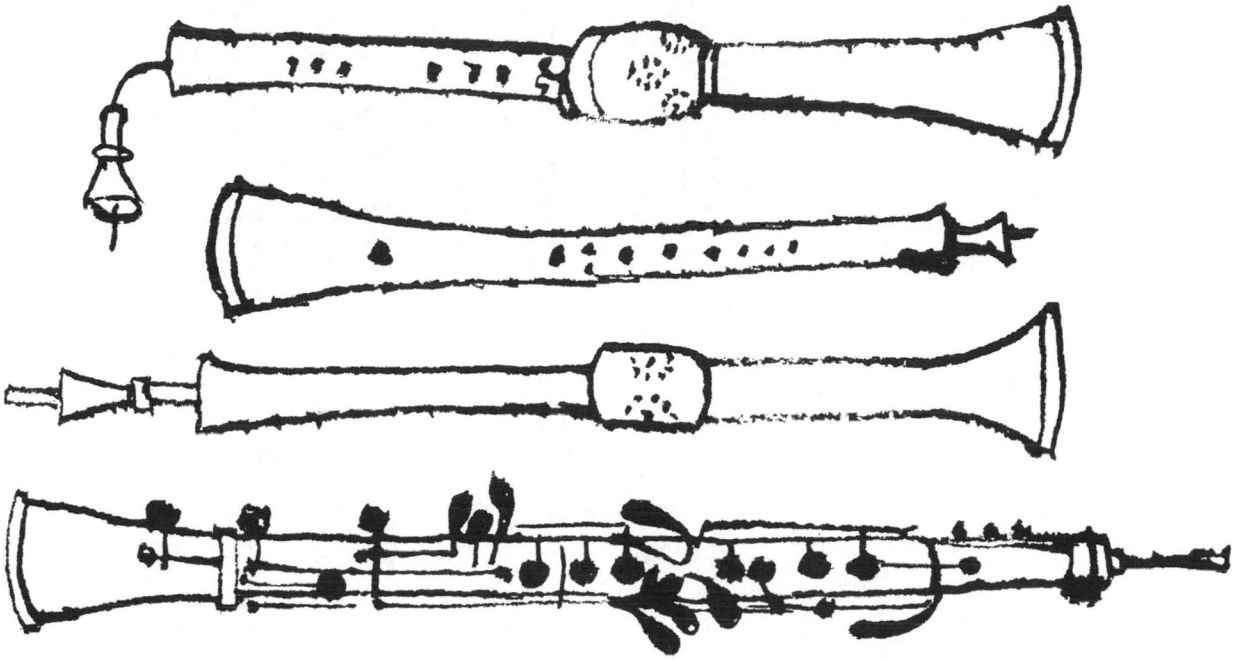

HOBNOB

BARLEY

DOG-EARED

HOPSCOTCH

WINDWARD

OAF

EGG

OBOE

NUTMEG

OBLONG

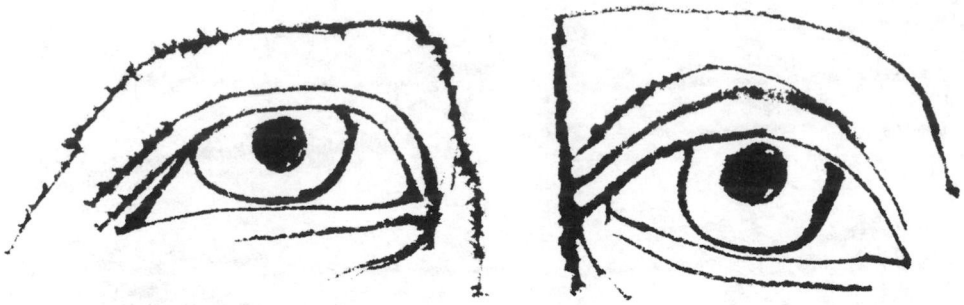

EYE

POOP

MINIM

LEVEL

KAYAK

MARRAM

DEIFIED REFER

WORDS THAT READ BOTH WAYS

DROWS

(read the wrong way round)

MULP

ANANAB

ROTSAC

OOBAGUB

OTAMOT

REZAGRATS

NOSAM

GUBDEB

WOLLEY

SQUISHY WORDS

(to be said when wet)

SQUIFF

SQUIDGE

SQUAMOUS

SQUINNY

SQUELCH

SQUASH

SQUEEGEE

SQUIRT

SQUAB

BUG WORDS

(to be said when grumpy)

HUMBUG

BUGBEAR

BUGABOO

BUGBANE

LADYBUG

BOGYBUG

BUGSEED

WORDS FOR TIMES OF DAY

(to be used where there are no clocks)

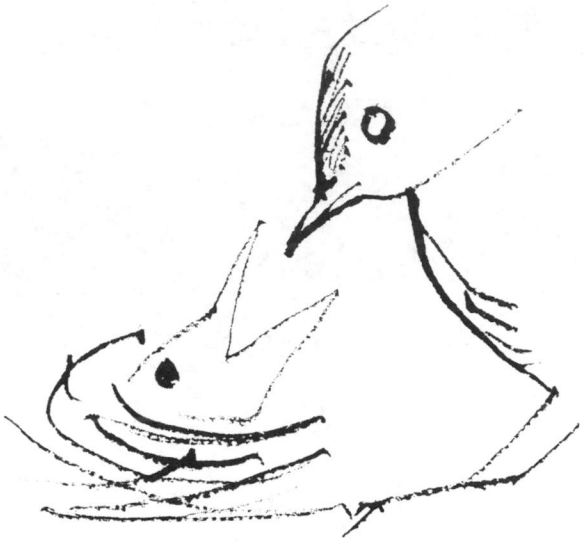

DAYPEEP

DAYSPRING

MERIDIAN

MAINDAY

DAYLIGONE

DIMITY

DEWFALL

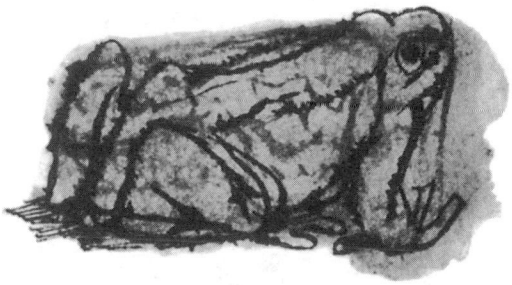

GLOAMING

DUSK

OWLCRY

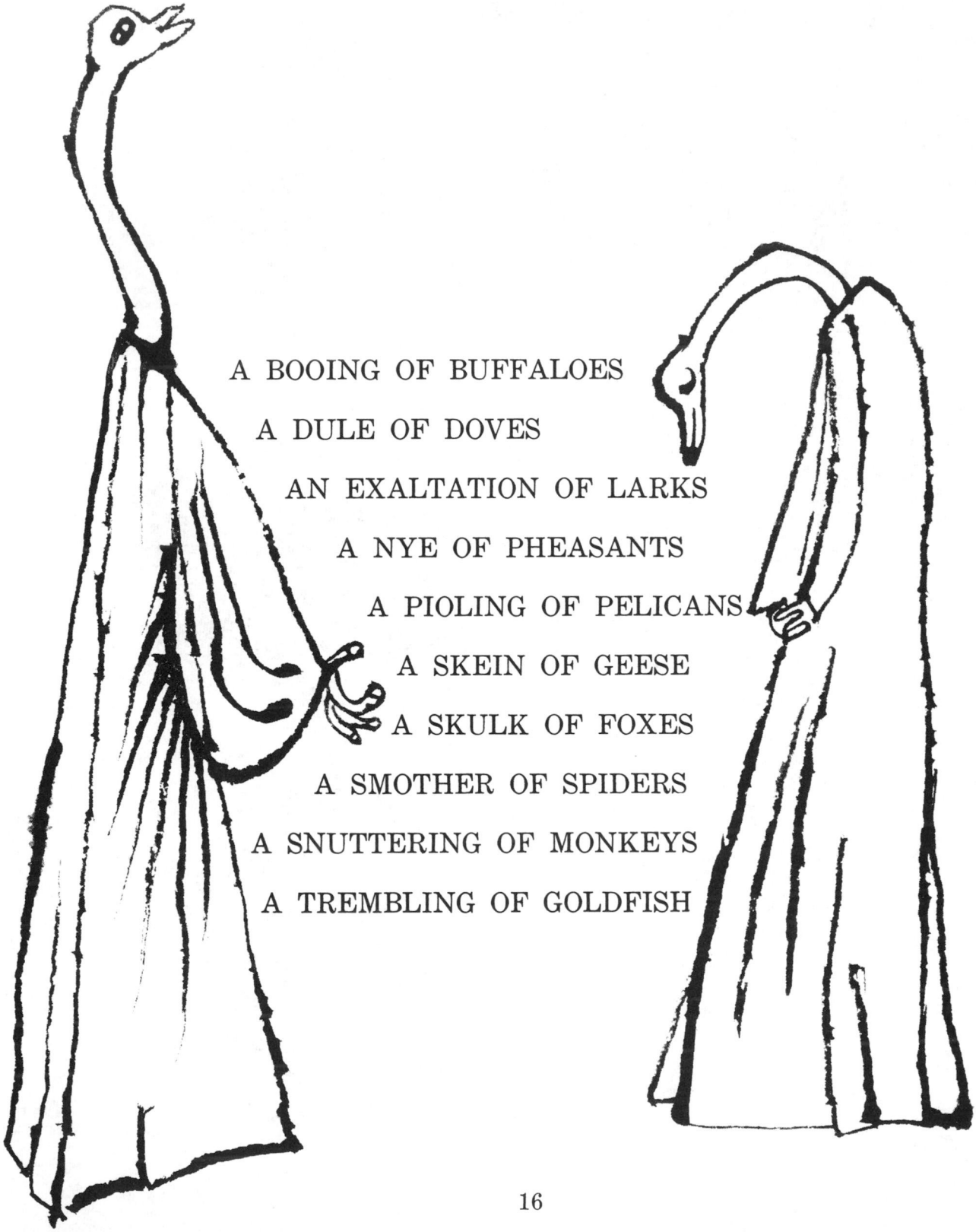

A BOOING OF BUFFALOES

A DULE OF DOVES

AN EXALTATION OF LARKS

A NYE OF PHEASANTS

A PIOLING OF PELICANS

A SKEIN OF GEESE

A SKULK OF FOXES

A SMOTHER OF SPIDERS

A SNUTTERING OF MONKEYS

A TREMBLING OF GOLDFISH

ODDS AND ENDS

A BLUNDER OF BOYS

A GIGGLE OF GIRLS

A CONSTERNATION OF MOTHERS

A GRUMBLING OF BUSES

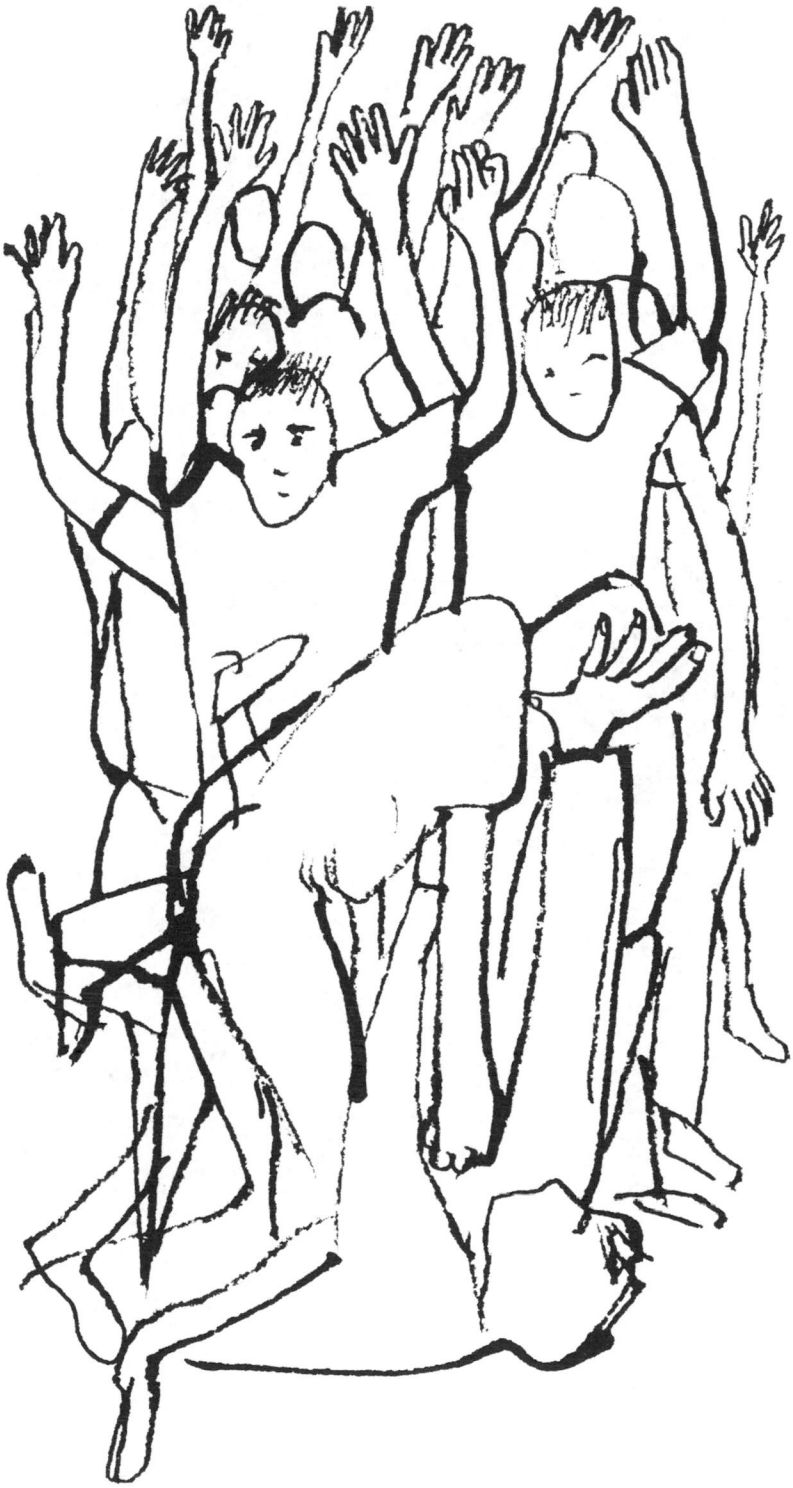

A HUMBUGGLE OF PACKAGES

A GUNDULUM OF GARBAGE CANS

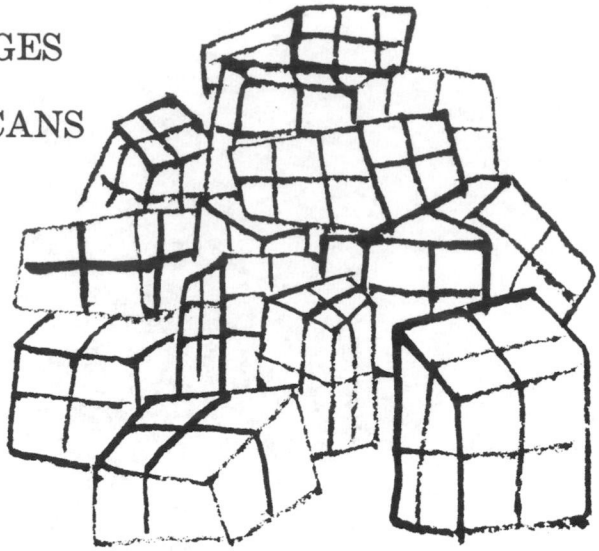

A SCRIBBITCH OF PAPERS

A TUMBLETELL OF CHURCH BELLS

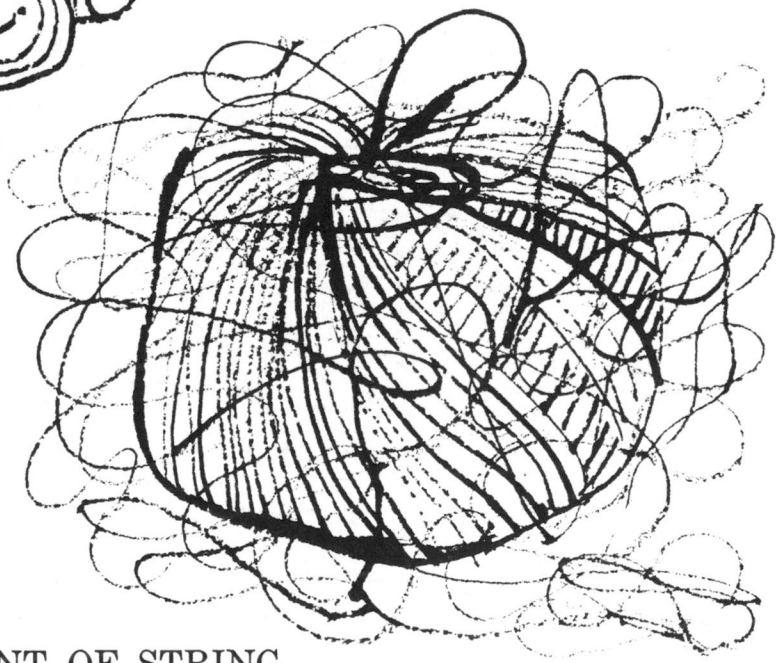

A SNIGGLEMENT OF STRING

A TRIBULATION OF CHILDREN

SOUNDS

PLOO is breaking your shoelace.

MRRAAOWL

is what

cats

really say.

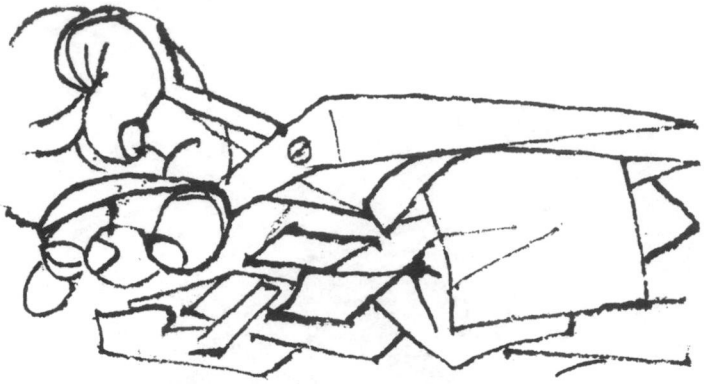

TRIS-TRAS

is scissors cutting paper.

KINCLUNK is a car

going over a manhole cover.

CROOMB is what pigeons

murmur to themselves.

PHLOOPH is sitting

suddenly on a cushion.

NYO-NYO is speaking with

your mouth full.

HARROWOLLOWORRAH is yawning.

PALOOP is the tap dripping in the bath.

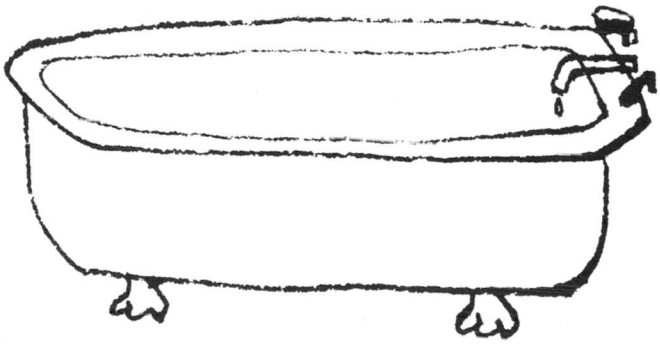

RAM TAM GEE PICKAGEE

is

feeling good.

It is most important to be a good namer, since it falls to all of us at some time or other to name anything from a canary to a castle, and since names generally have to last a long time. Here are some possible names for possible things, to give you ideas.

NAMES FOR ELEPHANTS

WILBUR ORMOND

BENDIGO BRUCE

McGRAW ROBERTSON

WENDELL TUBB DUFF

DEUTERONOMY

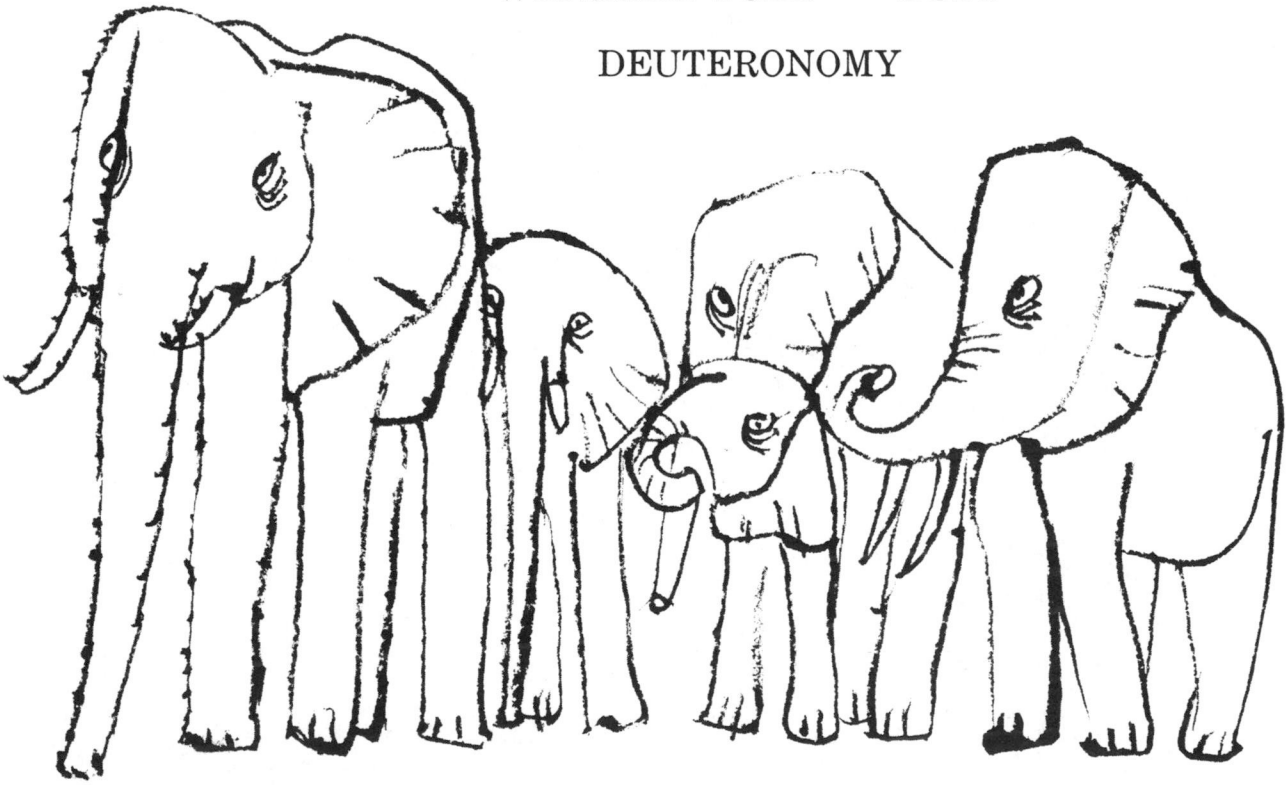

NAMES FOR CATS

SYBIL

CHESTER

LISSADEL

GRICE

MILDRED

FELICITY

ASTRID

JAMES BUDGE

TWEE

SINBAD

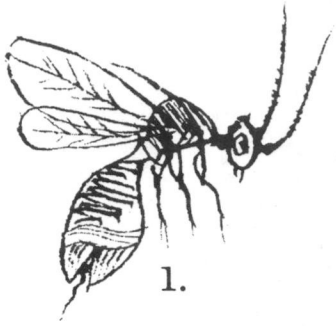

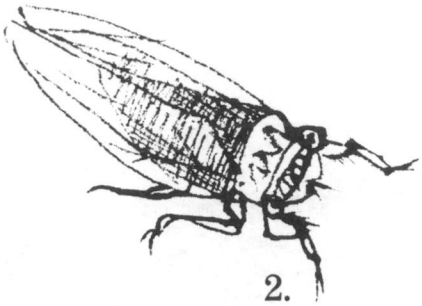

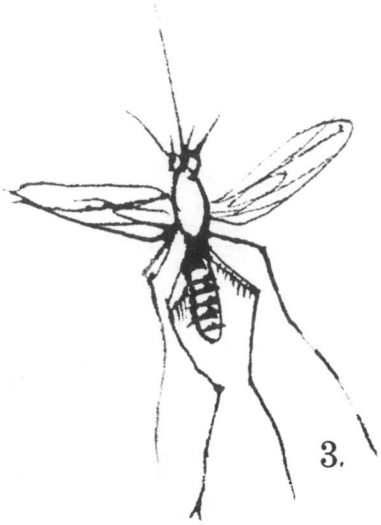

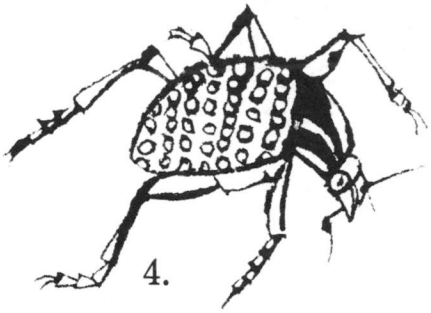

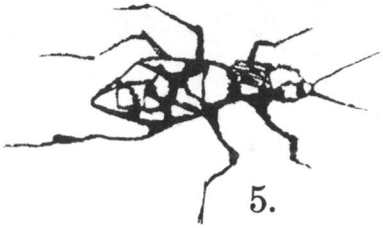

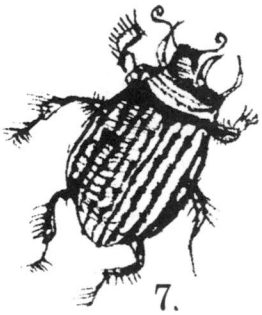

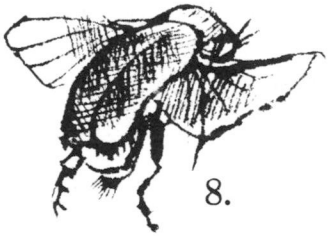

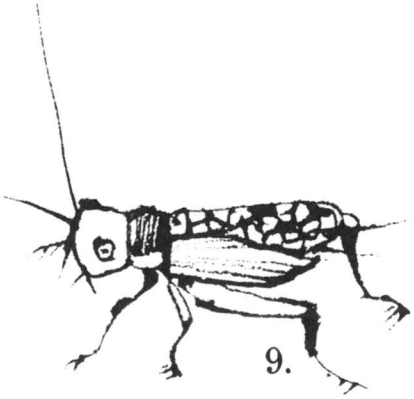

NAMES FOR INSECTS

1. TWILLITER
2. FLURR
3. TRISTRAM
4. LIMLET
5. TILLTIN
6. SUMMERSBY
7. THRIMM
8. LEGLIDDY
9. UGWOB

NAMES FOR WHALES

HUGH BLODGE BARNABY HAMISH

CHUMLEY MURDO CHAM OKUM SUMP

NAMES FOR HOUSES AND PLACES

HUGG HOUSE

THE BOBBINS

BROADMEADOWS

DEERSDEN

WINDYGATES

SMITHEREENS

HOPESHAWS

OLD HULLABALOO

SMIDGIN'S NOB

DRUMJARGON

LONG STILT LANE

THE SHIVERS

FROM THE ATLAS

PEE DEE

PARSNIP

TWEED

TOMBIGBEE

OUSE

SHOSHONE

CHINDWIN

CAM

OKEFINOKEE

APP

AAR

URR

RUDE NAMES FOR NITWITS

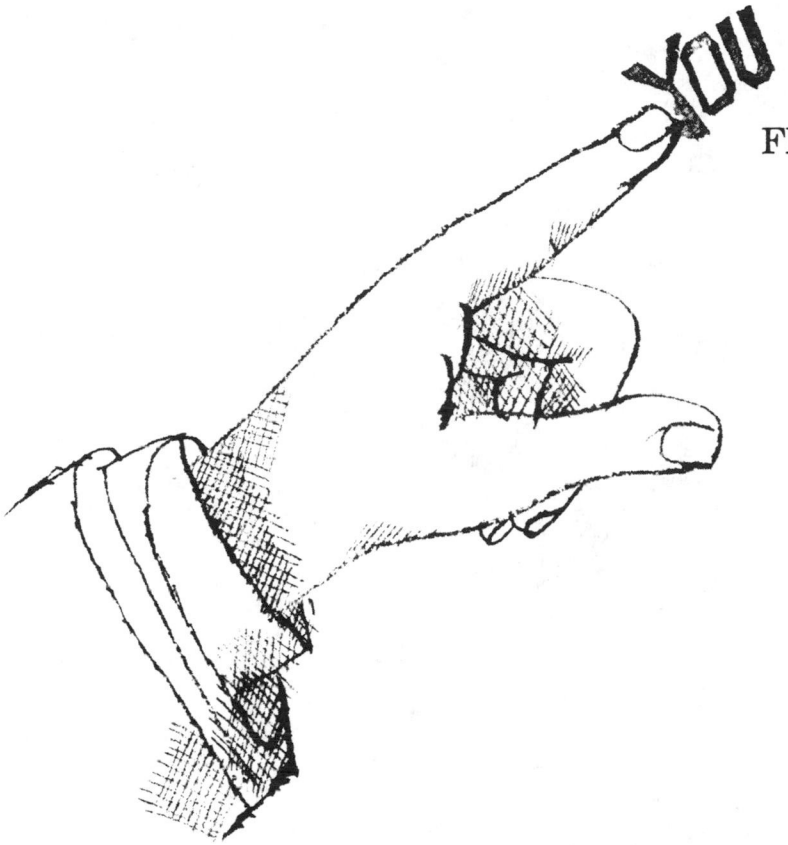

RAPSCALLION

FLIBBERTIGIBBET

FUSSBUDGET

COYSTRIL

TAYSTRIL

JOSKIN

BUMPKIN

CLOAF

CLODHOPPER

SLAMMERKIN

NAMES FOR THE FINGERS

(always starting with the thumb)

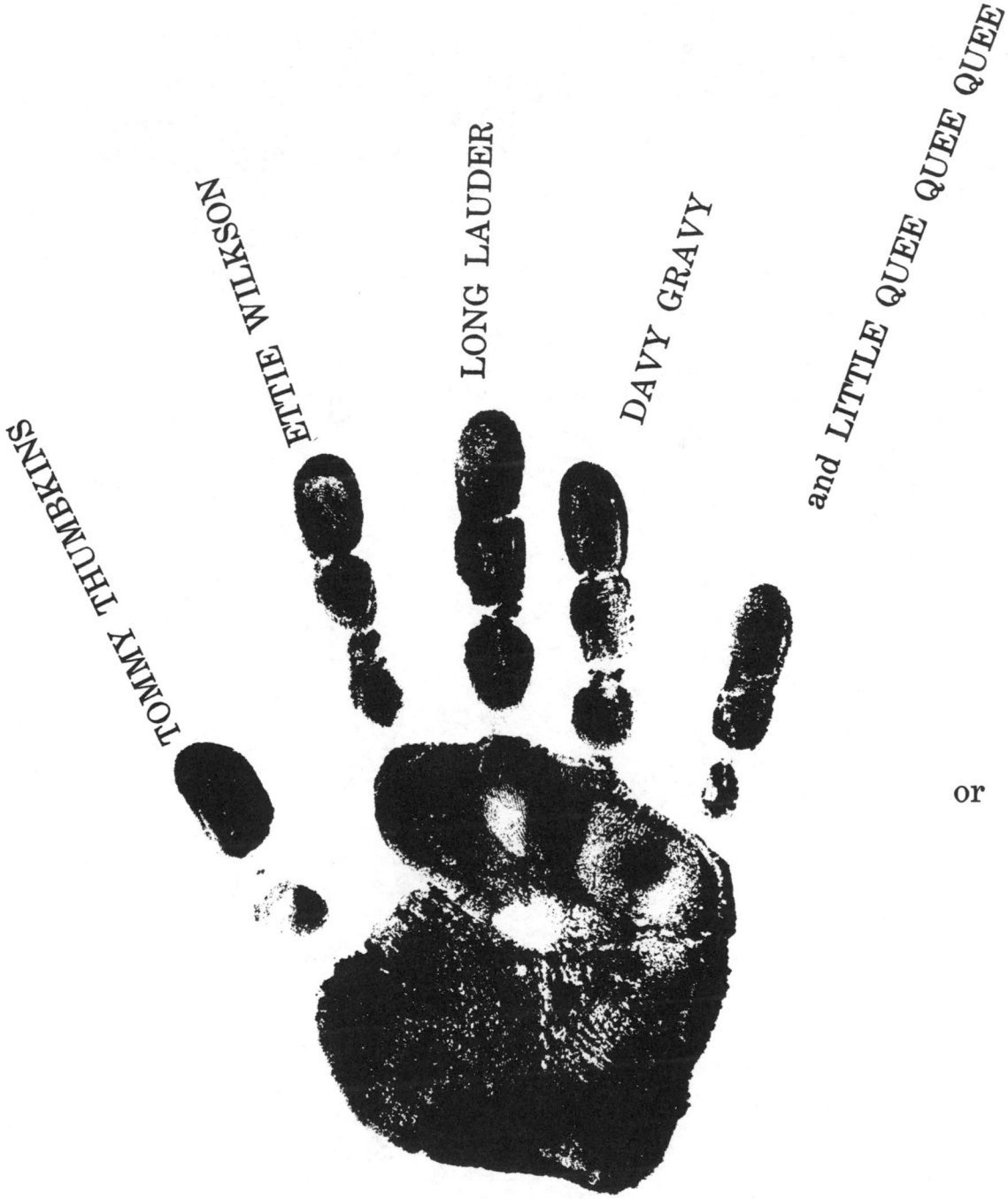

or

and LITTLE DIDO BONE
THE EARL OF ALMOND
SOBER JOHN
MINNIE MILTON
TIM SUNDRY

Ani's Hand

NAMES FOR TWINS

Each pair of twins,
rabbits or dogs,
children or frogs,
has to have names
that are almost the same
(to show that they're twins)
but are different too;
so here's what you do.

Find double words,
like Higgledy-Piggledy
(good names for pigs)

or Shilly and Shally
or Dilly and Dally
or Knick and Knack.

Namby and Pamby
are better for poodles;

Whing-Ding for swallows;
Misty and Moisty
and Wishy and Washy
especially for fish.

Call twin kittens
Inky and Pinky
or Helter and Skelter,
or Pell and Mell.
(It's easy to tell
they are twins if their names
have a humdrum sound.)

Crinkum and Crankum
are perfect for squirrels,
like Hanky and Panky
or Fiddle and Faddle;

but Mumbo and Jumbo
are mainly for elephants.
(Airy and Fairy
would never suit *them.*)
Willy and Nilly
will fit almost any twins.
Hubble and Bubble
or Hodge and Podge
or Roly and Poly
are mainly for fat twins.

Chitter and Chatter
or Jingle and Jangle
or Pitter and Patter,
of course, are for noisy twins.
Further than that,
there's Harum and Scarum,
or Hocus and Pocus,
or Heebie and Jeebie,
but these are peculiar,
and have to be used,
like Mixty and Maxty,
for very *odd* pairs. . . .
You see what begins
when you have to name twins.

If you get tired of counting *one, two, three,* make up your own numbers, as shepherds used to do when they had to count sheep day in, day out. You can try using these sets of words instead of numbers, when you have to count to ten.

OUNCE

DICE

TRICE

QUARTZ

QUINCE

SAGO

SERPENT

OXYGEN

NITROGEN

DENIM

INSTANT

DISTANT

TRYST

CATALYST

QUEST

SYCAMORE

SOPHOMORE

OCULIST

NOVELIST

DENTIST

ARCHERY

BUTCHERY

TREACHERY

TAPROOM

TOMB

SERMON

CINNAMON

APRON

NUNNERY

DENSITY

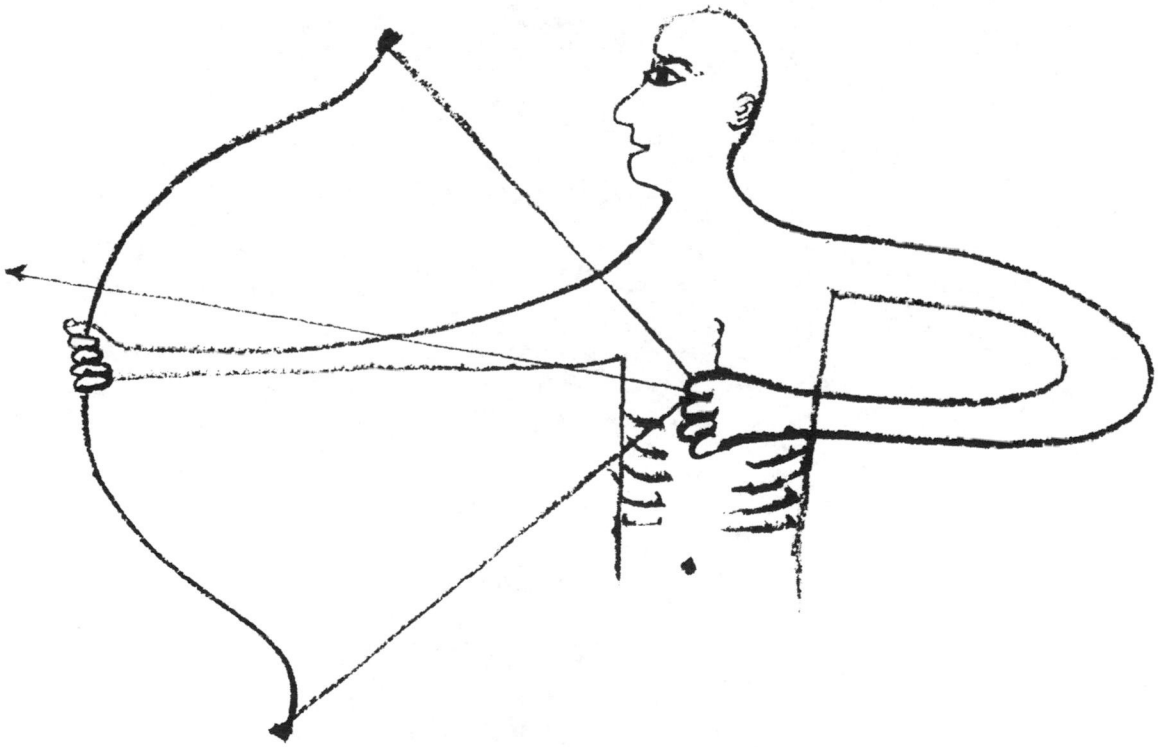

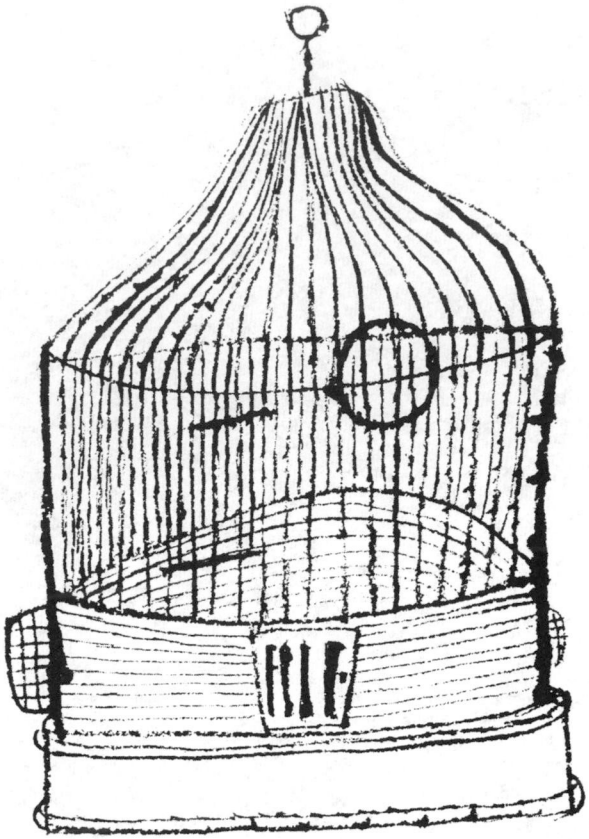

ACREAGE

BROKERAGE

CRIBBAGE

CARTHAGE

CAGE

SINK

SENTIMENT

OINTMENT

NUTMEG

DOOM

Here are some odd words, either forgotten or undiscovered, with which you can bamboozle almost anyone. They are arranged in Garlands which bring you always back to the beginning. Once you have been through them two or three times, you will be able to use them whenever you wish.

WHAT IS A TINGLE-AIREY?

A *tingle-airey* is a hand organ, usually played on the street by the turning of a handle, and often decorated with mother-of-pearl or *piddock* shells.

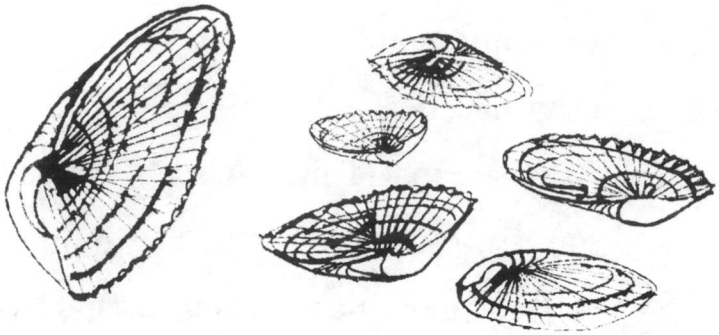

WHAT ARE PIDDOCKS?

Piddocks are little mollusks
which bore holes in rocks and wood,
or in the *breastsummers* of buildings.

WHAT IS A BREASTSUMMER?

A *breastsummer* is a great beam
supporting the weight of a wall,
and sometimes of a
gazebo above.

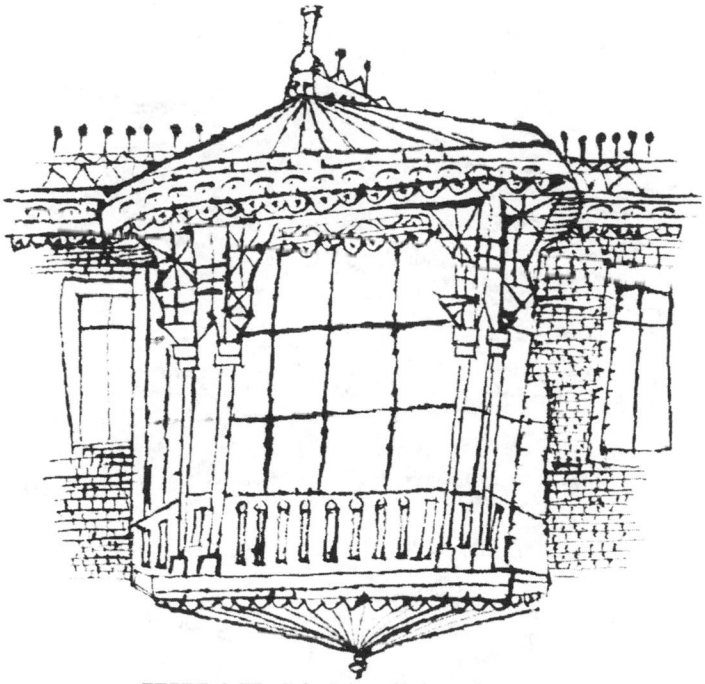

WHAT IS A GAZEBO?

A *gazebo* is a round balcony with large windows looking out on a view, often of ornamental gardens and *cotoneasters.*

WHAT IS A COTONEASTER?

A *cotoneaster* is a kind of flowering shrub, a favorite of *mumruffins.*

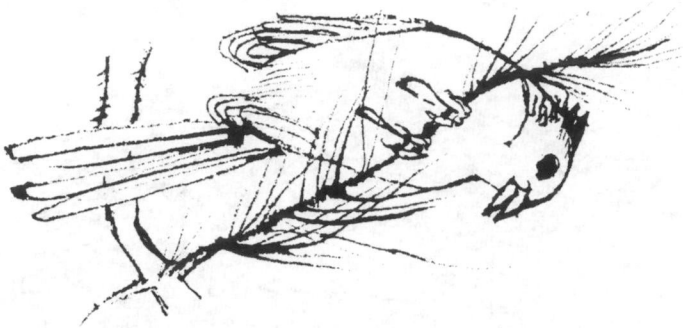

WHAT IS A MUMRUFFIN?

A *mumruffin* is a long-tailed tit which often visits bird tables in winter for its share of *pobbies.*

WHAT ARE POBBIES?

Pobbies are small pieces of bread *thrumbled* up with milk and fed to birds and baby animals.

WHAT IS THRUMBLED?

Thrumbled is squashed together. Ants thrumble round a piece of bread, and crowds in streets thrumble round *gongoozlers.*

WHAT IS A GONGOOZLER?

A *gongoozler* is an idle person who
is always stopping in the street
and staring at a curious object
like a *tingle-airey.*

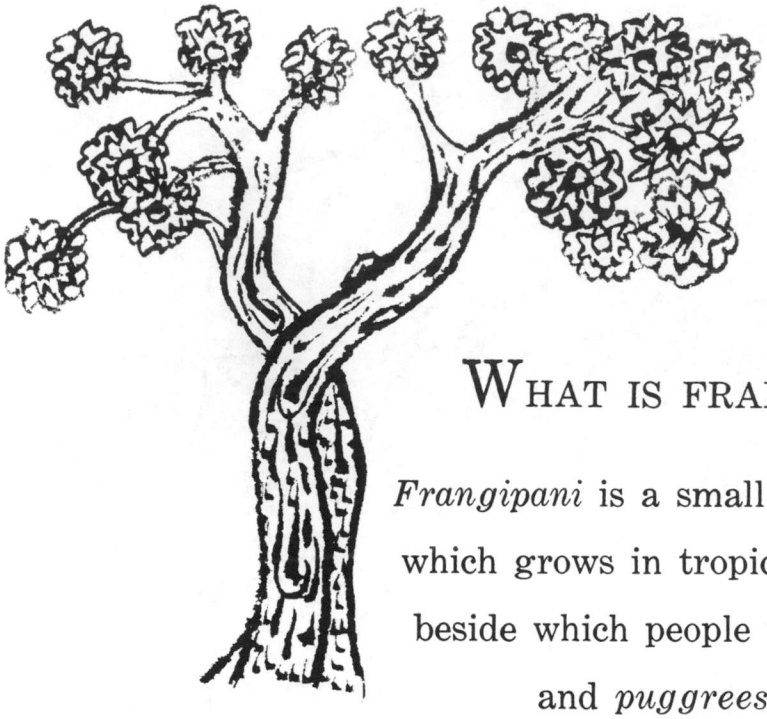

WHAT IS FRANGIPANI?

Frangipani is a small flowering tree which grows in tropical places, and beside which people wearing saris and *puggrees* walk.

WHAT IS A PUGGREE?

A *puggree* is a light scarf worn over a hat to protect the *paxwax* from the sun.

WHAT IS THE PAXWAX?

The *paxwax* is the tendon at the back of the neck which supports the head, and which flushes red when people are in a *tirrivee.*

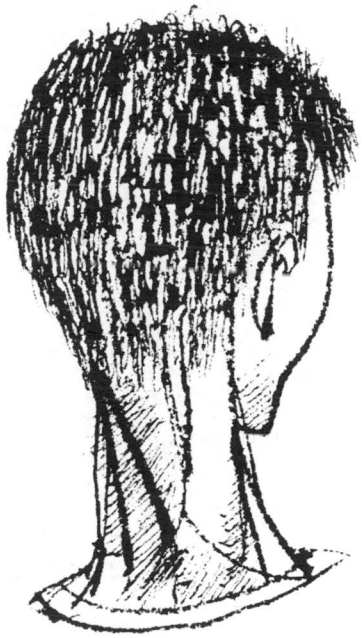

WHAT IS A TIRRIVEE?

A *tirrivee* is a temper. Mothers go into a tirrivee over the *jiggery-pokery* of children.

WHAT IS JIGGERY-POKERY?

Jiggery-pokery is trickery or mischief or hanky-panky on the part of children, such as pretending to be deaf or teasing a *Tantony.*

WHAT IS A TANTONY? A *Tantony* is the smallest pig in a litter, so called after Saint Anthony, the patron saint of swineherds. Small creatures are usually given special names, like kittens or cygnets or *quicklings*.

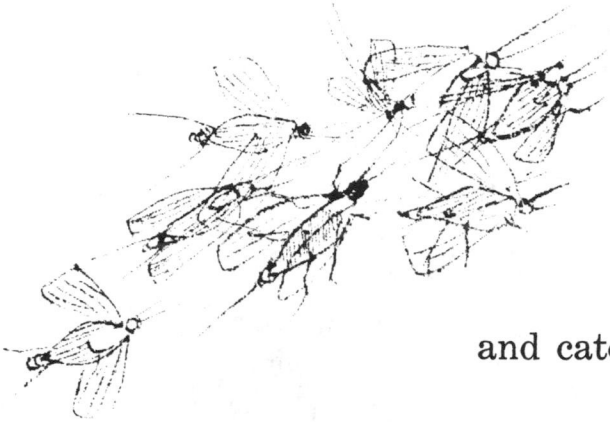

WHAT ARE QUICKLINGS?

Quicklings are young insects which in summer dance in the air in clouds and catch the light, looking like *moonglade*.

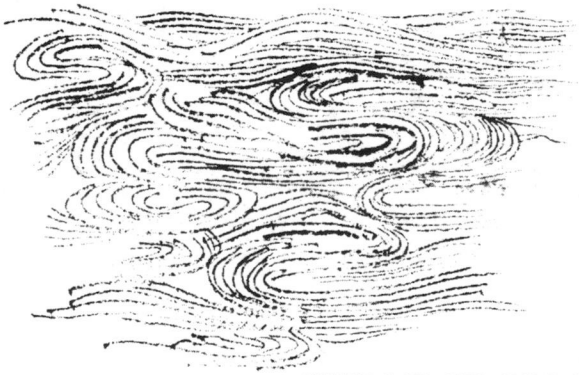

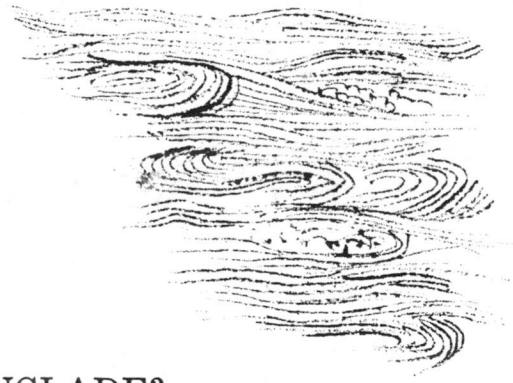

WHAT IS MOONGLADE?

Moonglade is the track of dancing broken light left on the sea at *dimity* by the moon.

WHAT IS DIMITY?

Dimity, besides being a fine cotton fabric, is the time of day when the daylight dims, the time when, in hot countries, men and women walk in the coolth beside the *frangipani.*

WHAT IS A HAMBURGLER?

A *hamburgler* is a hamburger which you creep downstairs and eat in the middle of the night when you wake up hungry. *Mim* people never eat hamburglers.

WHAT ARE MIM PEOPLE?

Mim people are very proper people who always sit with their fingertips together and their lips pursed tight, who always do the right thing, and who disapprove. Mim people have *worgs* in their gardens.

WHAT IS A WORG?

A *worg* is a plant which never grows. There is practically always one worg in a row of plants. You can tell it by the *gnurr* on its leaves.

WHAT IS GNURR?

GNURR is the substance which collects after periods of time in the bottom of pockets or in the cuffs of trousers. Gnurr is a smaller variety of *oosse.*

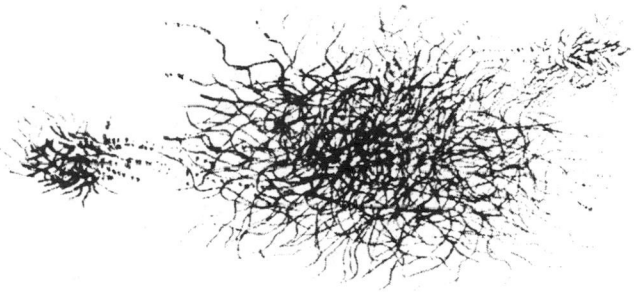

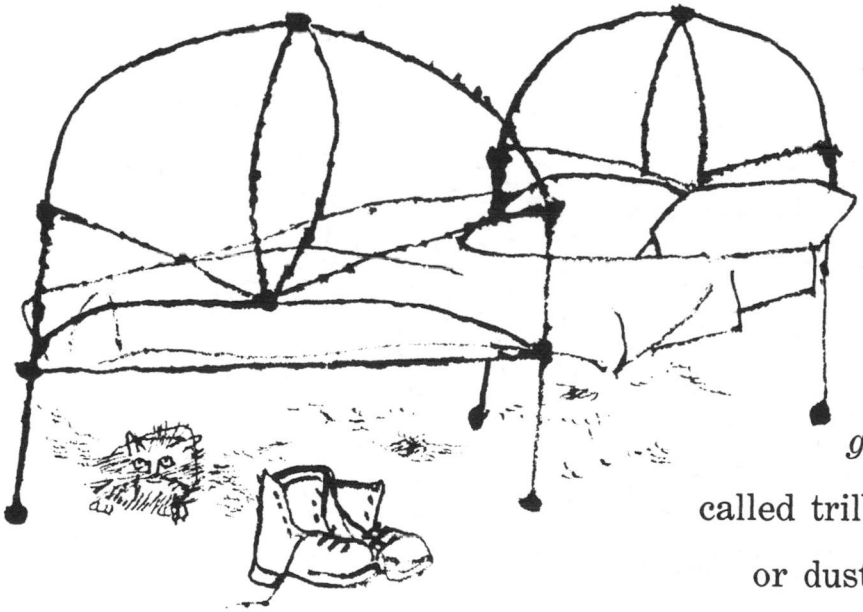

WHAT IS OOSSE?

OOSSE is the airy furry stuff that ultimately gathers under beds and *gonomonies.* It is also called trilbies, kittens, or dust-bunnies.

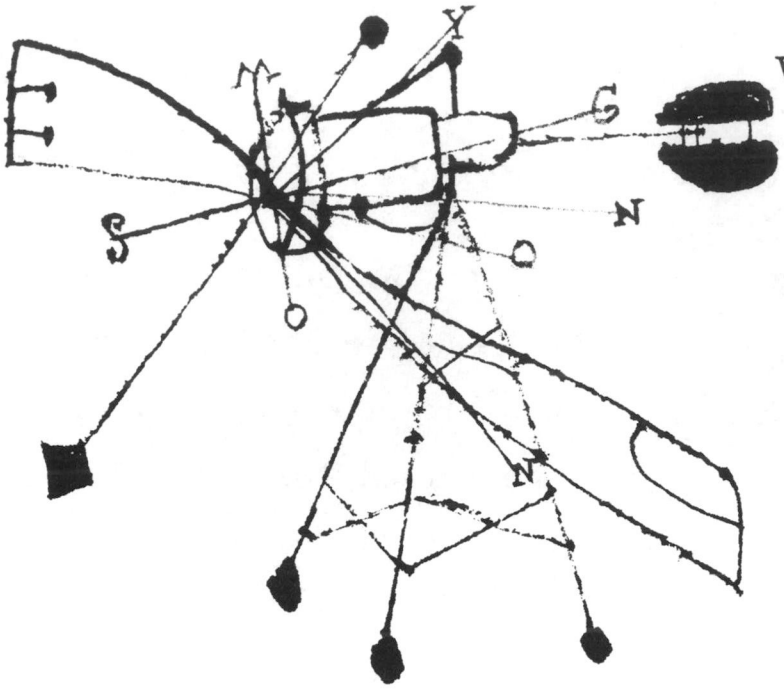

WHAT IS A GONOMONY?

A *gonomony* is any strange object that is difficult to name, that is curiously unlike anything else, and that serves no useful purpose. Gonomonies abound in the houses of *glots.*

WHAT IS A GLOT?

A *glot* is a person who cannot bear to waste anything, who stuffs his attic full of treasures which nobody else wants, and who always eats the last chocolate in the box. Glots can be recognized by the *poose* on their noses.

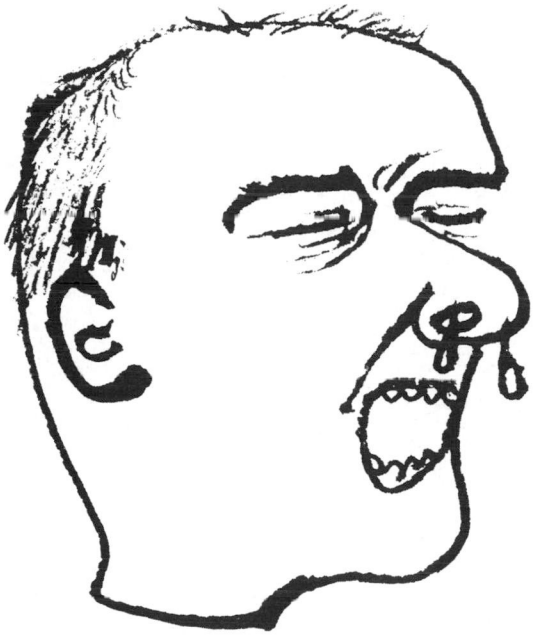

WHAT IS A POOSE?

A *poose* is a drop which stays on the end of the nose and glistens. It happens to ordinary people when they have colds, or when they come out of the sea for a *chittering-bite.*

WHAT IS A CHITTERING-BITE?

A *chittering-bite* is a snack eaten after a cold swim to keep the teeth from chattering. It may consist of anything from an apple to a piece of leftover *hamburgler.*

CURIOSITIES

If you want to call for silence, say

MUMBUDGET

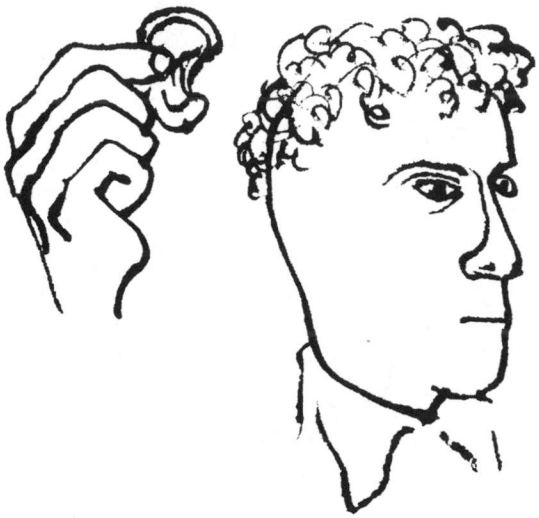

If you want to change the subject, say

PONSONBY

If you want to stop a game that you are playing, say

BARLEY PAX KING'S X

KING'S RANSOM FINS

KEYS UNCLE

or

CRIK-CRAK

And if someone tells
you something
you don't believe,
look at him steadily
and say
FIRKYDOODLE
FUDGE
or
QUOZ

ALASTAIR REID is a poet, translator, essayist, and scholar of Latin American literature. He has been on the staff of *The New Yorker* since 1959 and has translated works by Pablo Neruda and Jorge Luis Borges. Among his many books for children are *A Balloon for a Blunderbuss* and *I Keep Changing* (illustrated by Bob Gill) and *Supposing* (illustrated by Abe Birnbaum). In 2008 he published two career-spanning collections of work, *Inside Out: Selected Poetry and Translations* and *Outside In: Selected Prose*.

BEN SHAHN (1898–1969) was a painter, muralist, printmaker, and illustrator. He was best known for his socially and politically informed artwork, including a famous series of paintings depicting the trial of the anarchists Sacco and Vanzetti. His 1956 Charles Eliot Norton lectures were collected and published as *The Shape of Content*, and he illustrated numerous books of poetry. *Ounce Dice Trice* is the only book he illustrated that was written specifically for children.

TITLES IN THE NEW YORK REVIEW CHILDREN'S COLLECTION

ESTHER AVERILL
Captains of the City Streets
The Hotel Cat
Jenny and the Cat Club
Jenny Goes to Sea
Jenny's Birthday Book
Jenny's Moonlight Adventure
The School for Cats

JAMES CLOYD BOWMAN *and* LAURA BANNON
Pecos Bill: The Greatest Cowboy of All Time

SHEILA BURNFORD
Bel Ria: Dog of War

DINO BUZZATI
The Bears' Famous Invasion of Sicily

INGRI *and* EDGAR PARIN D'AULAIRE
D'Aulaires' Book of Animals
D'Aulaires' Book of Norse Myths
D'Aulaires' Book of Trolls
Foxie: The Singing Dog
The Terrible Troll-Bird
Too Big
The Two Cars

EILÍS DILLON
The Island of Horses
The Lost Island

ELEANOR FARJEON
The Little Bookroom

PENELOPE FARMER
Charlotte Sometimes

RUMER GODDEN
An Episode of Sparrows
The Mousewife

LUCRETIA P. HALE
The Peterkin Papers

RUTH KRAUSS *and* MARC SIMONT
The Backward Day

MUNRO LEAF *and* ROBERT LAWSON
Wee Gillis

NORMAN LINDSAY
The Magic Pudding

ERIC LINKLATER
The Wind on the Moon

J. P. MARTIN *and* QUENTIN BLAKE
Uncle
Uncle Cleans Up

JOHN MASEFIELD
The Box of Delights
The Midnight Folk

E. NESBIT
The House of Arden

BARBARA SLEIGH
Carbonel: The King of the Cats
The Kingdom of Carbonel

JAMES THURBER *and* MARC SIMONT
The 13 Clocks
The Wonderful O

T. H. WHITE
Mistress Masham's Repose

REINER ZIMNIK
The Bear and the People
The Crane